NICOLE SIMON

The Mystery at Bakers Inn

A Baking Mystery

Copyright © 2023 by Nicole Simon

All rights reserved. No part of this publication may be reproduced, stored or transmitted in any form or by any means, electronic, mechanical, photocopying, recording, scanning, or otherwise without written permission from the publisher. It is illegal to copy this book, post it to a website, or distribute it by any other means without permission.

Copyright 2023 - All rights reserved.

The content contained within this book may not be reproduced, duplicated or transmitted without direct written permission from the author or the publisher.

Under no circumstances will any blame or legal responsibility be held against the publisher, or author, for any damages, reparation, or monetary loss due to the information contained within this book, either directly or indirectly.

Legal Notice:

This book is copyright protected. It is only for personal use. You cannot amend, distribute, sell, use, quote or paraphrase any part, or the content within this book, without the consent of the author or publisher.

Disclaimer Notice:

Please note the information contained within this document is for educational and entertainment purposes only. All effort has been executed to present accurate, up to date, reliable, complete information. No warranties of any kind are declared or implied. Readers acknowledge that the author is not engaged in the rendering of legal, financial, medical or professional advice. The content within this book has been derived from various sources. Please consult a licensed professional before attempting any techniques outlined in this book.

By reading this document, the reader agrees that under no circumstances is the author responsible for any losses, direct or indirect, that are incurred as a result of the use of the information contained within this document, including, but not limited to, errors, omissions, or inaccuracies.

First edition

This book was professionally typeset on Reedsy.
Find out more at reedsy.com

Contents

Chapter 1

The blueberry muffins smelled delicious, fresh from the oven. Diana closed her eyes and deeply inhaled the sweet, warm aroma.

"You—my little magnificent muffins—are baked to perfection!" She said to herself with a joyful giggle.

She sat down the two trays on a cooling rack and checked the time on the massive wooden clock that hung on the white wall. She loved the character it added to the kitchen.

"Almost 7 o'clock. Our guests will be coming down for breakfast soon, Peaches," chirped Diana to her plump tabby cat, who was basking in the first rays of morning sunshine pouring through the glass window.

Diana shuffled around the kitchen excitedly, trying to ensure that everything was perfectly prepared for her guests. She had a warm, hospitable personality and possessed remarkable wit and charm, which allowed her to blend in and socialize with different types of people.

The scent of the strong coffee she brewed permeated the air, and the sound of eggs sizzling in the pan gave a cozy ambiance to the morning atmosphere.

Her dark hair cascaded over her shoulders as she leaned in to carefully arrange the fruit platters and place the pancakes on China plates.

Breakfast at Bakers Inn was always scrumptious. Diana wanted to ensure that her guests started their day with a filling meal.

"I think we're just about ready, Peaches," she said, smiling satisfactorily with her hands on her hips.

She carried all the items to the dining area, which caught the bright rays of sunlight. Diana moved quickly and with purpose. Her petite frame and swift movements mimicked that of a lady half her age.

As she sat down the last napkin, she heard shuffling from atop the staircase. Diana smiled warmly.

"Good morning," she beamed as she noticed the couple making their way down. "Did you sleep well?"

These were first-time guests, and she wanted to make a good impression.

"Ah, top of the morning to you, Dear." Mrs. Johnson replied. Her husband just responded with a quiet nod while touching the tip of his hat in acknowledgment.

Diana led the couple into the dining area. Mrs. Johnson was a slim and rather stern-looking woman. Her husband hadn't said much since checking in but seemed to be a pleasant fellow. The Johnsons appeared to be at least 20 years Diana's senior but still quite agile.

She wondered what it must feel like to grow old with a partner. Diana had never married. Her life before Bakers Inn was a busy one. She was a detective for many years and retired early for a slower-paced lifestyle.

Her passion for baking led her to convert her inherited Midwest home into a bed and breakfast. Running her own business brought her peace and a sense of accomplishment, but there was still a spark for sleuthing left in her.

Sometimes the longing to go back to that edgy career overwhelmed her, but she busied herself with her daily duties until the feelings faded.

Mr. Johnson sat down at the table and inspected the surroundings carefully. It was adorned with tasteful decor and simple lace curtains, which made the room feel light and cheerful.

Mrs. Johnson paged through a pamphlet filled with local attractions. She began chattering away and asking various rhetorical questions about the region. Mr. Johnson smiled in response to his wife's animated excitement.

Soon more guests started making their way down, and before long, the room was filled with sounds of laughter and gleeful chatter.

Diana enjoyed the noise and made her way from table to table, checking if all her patrons were happy.

"Do you know much about the history of this town?" a young woman named Amy asked as Diana refilled her coffee.

Diana paused for a moment and thought carefully.

"Oh, yes!" said Amy again. "And what are the pool hours?"

Relieved by the follow-up question, Diana responded. "While you are allowed to access the pool at all times, I only ask that you all respect my neighbors and their right to a peaceful night's rest!"

"Does that mean no midnight splashing for us young folk?" Mr. Johnson quipped after overhearing the rules about the pool.

Diana and Amy giggled.

"Well, as long as no one's skinny dipping, I suppose it will be fine," Diana responded with a chuckle. "Anything else?"

"I have a question," began Mrs. Johnson, clearing her throat and maintaining a firm frown. "What can you tell us about the legend of Old Smithy and the abandoned goldmine?"

Diana furrowed her brows. She didn't like to talk about the town's history. These were just myths anyway, but somehow talking about it made the old detective feel uneasy.

The room grew silent, and all eyes were on her, eager for a response to the intriguing question.

She kept her demeanor calm as she explained the legend. "In all honesty," began Diana carefully, "I don't know too much about the legend. It dates back many decades ago."

"Well, what snippets do you know about it?" Amy inquired eagerly.

Diana smiled and said, "From what I understand, rumors state that a miner hid an enormous treasure but died in a tragic accident while working, preventing him from ever recovering it."

"How did he pass away?" asked Elliot, whipping out a small notebook and pen. He seemed the studious type and couldn't be much older than 24. "Did the cave collapse?" he continued, "Was there erosion evidence of geological weathering in the mine?"

"Ohhh, is the cave haunted?" asked Amy, giggling and pretending to shiver. "Spooky!"

"Are there any speculations as to where the treasure may be?" asked Mr. Johnson.

Diana put her hands up, laughing. "Whoa there! Again, I'm not very familiar with the complete story."

The guests seemed disappointed by her answer.

"Perhaps some of you might be interested in visiting? I believe I have the address listed under hotspots in each of your pamphlets. There are weekly tours available," Diana informed the group.

"I would find that enjoyable," agreed Elliot.

"As would we!" added Mr. Johnson, and his wife nodded in approval.

Diana was happy to steer the conversation to the mine tours instead of the tale that haunted the town. Although so much time had passed, the eerie legend still played a role in the town's reputation.

She made her way to a table at the back of the dining area. It was the only spot in the room that didn't receive any light.

"More coffee Mr. Franklin?" Diana asked.

Mr. Franklin, who had been almost unnoticeable, nodded slowly as if he was contemplating. After a moment, he glanced at Mrs. Johnson curiously, narrowed his eyes, and suddenly seemed to shift his thoughts.

"I believe I could also participate," he said finally.

Diana smiled as she refilled his mug.

He looked up before taking a sip of coffee. "You never know what secrets may be uncovered on this vacation."

Diana shook her head and laughed. "It's just an old myth."

Her guests seemed quite happy to chatter about the mine and town history. Soon she heard the door creaking open in the lobby, and her two rescue dogs ran toward her.

Her assistant Bobby was there to start his shift after taking the pups for their morning walk.

"Good morning, you two rascals. Were you good to Bobby?" Diana greeted.

"They're full of energy," Bobby replied. "Are there any muffins left?"

Diana nodded as she rubbed Bobby's shoulder reassuringly.

"Alright, everybody, I'm off! If you need anything, Bobby here will assist you. I'll see you all at lunch," Diana announced as she exited the room.

Bobby smiled and waved at the guests.

As her guests all continued to get to know each other, Diana stepped back into her kitchen and started preparing a luxurious chocolate cake she had planned for dessert later that evening. While she mumbled the ingredients and measurements to herself, her mind bubbled with questions.

Why was there so much interest in that old goldmine suddenly? It's been investigated before. Locals confirmed it to be a legend.

DING!

Diana picked up her phone and saw a message from her closest friend, Miriam.

Miriam: Hey there! Just checking in to see how your day is going. Things are slow here. Are you too busy for a call?

Diana called Miriam.

"Hello?" answered Miriam.

"Hi! I got your message. I'm just prepping some cake. I can talk for a bit."

"Fantastic! How is everything going?"

"A few ups and a few downs, I guess. Most of the guests seemed nice, and they certainly enjoyed the muffins—I'm sorry I haven't even asked how things are on your side?"

Miriam laughed. "No worries. I'm just on a case, as usual. There have been some interesting developments regarding a certain pop singer. I can't say more, though."

Diana felt a familiar pang of curiosity. It had always been Diana's dream to convert her grandparents' massive, Western home into a Bed and Breakfast, but she never anticipated missing sleuthing so much.

Her detective career was a demanding one. She hadn't had the time to find love, let alone start a family. After working alongside her partner Miriam for over 30 years on the force, Diana felt ready to retire from the field and put everything into her dream.

Suddenly she wasn't so sure that this was the right decision.

"I get it. Top secret stuff, not for the eyes and ears of a regular civilian like myself," Diana teased.

Miriam giggled.

"To be honest, I'm starting to miss the field," Diana confessed.

Miriam replied, "I thought you were happy, Di?"

"I mean, I am..." Diana stammered. "I have my rescue pups, my cats, my guests. It's fulfilling, but there's a strange longing..." she trailed off.

"I understand, it's a catch-22. You're torn between what you've always done, what you excel at, and your peaceful dream."

"Exactly, Miriam. I feel almost restless to a degree. We can talk about this more later. I have to get the lunch menu prepared before Bobby leaves."

"Sure, I'll let you go now. I've got to run, too. Talk to you later!" said Miriam.

Diana set her phone down on the counter and smiled to herself.

She popped the cake in the oven and took out a massive recipe book, and paged through it.

"Ah yes, lemon meringue pie. What do you think, Peaches?" Diana asked her tabby cat enthusiastically.

Of all her pets, Peaches loved keeping her company in the kitchen the most.

Diana carefully set aside the ingredients and started making the crust of the pie.

A simple base would do. Then she worked on the filling of eggs, condensed milk, and lemon juice. Diana wanted her flavors to linger in the tastebuds, so she squeezed her own juice and zested the same lemon.

Finally, she made the meringue. Beautiful stiff peaks formed in her mixing bowl. She put it all together and popped it in the oven.

"Hmmm. What else shall we make?" she pondered out loud.

Soon she found a recipe for rich tomato soup and a decadent savory quiche that would complement each other.

Feeling quite ambitious, she also decided to bake fresh baguettes and a vibrant salad.

Her hands moved with skillful grace as she put the meal together. A blend of tantalizing aromas wafted around the kitchen, and soon everything was ready to be served.

She smiled as she wiped the sweat off her brow.

She headed to the dining area with trays of food and decided to serve lunch in a buffet style. She stacked plates and cups, and cutlery along with napkins.

She had just finished setting the centerpiece, a large vase with daisies, when the Johnson's made their way into the dining area.

"Please feel free to help yourselves to lunch," Diana chimed. "There's tomato soup, quiche, as well as fresh baguettes and salad. And, for dessert, I'll be bringing out lemon meringue pie."

"Oooh. I do love a good meringue pie," Mr. Johnson answered jovially.

"Ah, but first we must tuck into the quiche," Mrs. Johnson responded. "Where did you learn how to cook, Dear? This morning's breakfast was spectacular."

Diana smiled. "My mother and my grandmother both loved to cook and taught me everything they knew when I was growing up."

"That's wonderful!" Mr. Johnson piped in while munching down some quiche.

Soon most of the guests were happily serving themselves and enjoying their meals. Everyone was in attendance except Amy.

Chapter 2

Amy spent most of the afternoon and early evening exploring the town. It was a warm yet breezy Tuesday, perfect for a stroll.

The last rays of sunlight were fading into the purple and orange hues of dusk when she decided to make her way back to the cozy B&B. As she opened the front door, tantalizing aromas immediately grabbed her attention.

She smiled, knowing that a feast awaited her. Glancing at her watch, she knew Diana would be serving dinner within the hour.

She ran upstairs for a quick shower first. As she reached the top of the stairs, she bumped into Bobby. He was adjusting a painting in the lobby that seemed to go crooked on its own.

"Hello," She greeted confidently as she brushed past him.

"Oh, hi. We missed you at lunch," Bobby replied.

"Oh yeah, I was too excited to stop by for a meal," Amy replied. "I went on the mine tour and found out so much about the Old Smithy legend. I think I may even be on track to find his treasure."

Bobby smiled politely, "Good luck to you then."

She smiled back, and then she left him to finish up with the painting.

When she finally made her way down for dinner, she found that Diana had laid out quite the spread.

It was much more elaborate than anyone could expect from a small-town B&B. Once again, Diana served her feast buffet style.

She had Bobby replace the fresh flower centerpiece from lunch with dainty, vanilla-scented candles, each shielded with a glass cover. The dim lighting gave the room an almost romantic atmosphere.

Only Elliot had begun tucking into his meal. The rest of the guests were still making their way down.

Amy noticed him and asked, "Wow. What has she decided to spoil us with this evening?"

Elliot looked up as he placed a spoonful of mashed potatoes in his mouth. He beckoned to the feast behind him. "A feast fit for royalty. Hurry up and get some before I go back for seconds," He joked.

Amy giggled politely as she grabbed a plate.

On the one side of the table was an array of vegetables, such as roasted parsnips and beets, creamed spinach, earthy greens, mashed potatoes, and steamed cauliflower.

On the other was an assortment of flaky pastries and a rather large raspberry and almond tart. There were also various bread options, including one topped with sundried tomatoes and basil.

At the center of the table, Diana had placed the main attractions of the meal, a perfectly seared rack of lamb and a display of delicious chicken breasts.

"Good evening, everyone," Diana greeted as she placed a few more pastries on the table.

The guests greeted back, and soft chatter ensued.

"Diana, you won't believe all the information I dug up about Old Smithy today." Amy chattered excitedly while the old detective filled the punch.

Everyone quietened down and listened intently at the mention of Old Smithy. "What did you find out, Dear?" Diana questioned politely.

"Well, I went on the mine tour. The guide admitted that there really was a miner named Smith, and he also mentioned that his family still lives in town."

"Did he give you an address?" Asked Elliot.

"Not exactly, but I poked around a bit and found out that there's a link between Old Smithy's family and this very property," Amy enunciated the last three words as if she'd found an intriguing mystery.

"Ah, pish posh," Diana dismissed the comment.

"It's true," Amy insisted. "But his family didn't enjoy me asking so many questions, so I left before I overstayed my welcome." She shrugged.

Diana gasped in shock. "Amy, you did not go and interrogate that family, did you?"

"It wasn't an interrogation," Amy responded. "I just told them I was curious about the miner who made this town famous several decades ago."

Diana sighed and shook her head.

"I'll be upstairs filling your minibars if anyone needs me. I'll be back to clear the tables when I'm done," Diana announced before heading upstairs.

The guests continued chatting about the mine, and Amy was more than happy to fill everyone in on what she'd discovered.

"AAAAAAAAH!" Diana's voice broke into a piercing scream from upstairs.

Everyone's eyes darted to the stairs.

"Diana, are you alright?" Mr. Franklin asked in a raised voice so she might hear him.

When no response came, he got up from his table and went to inspect the situation.

Once he got there, he observed that the window was wide open, and Diana stood flustered before a set of muddy footprints on the carpet.

It was a peculiar sight; the prints started at the window and stopped right in the middle of the upstairs lobby.

"I'm not sure if this is a burglary?" Diana stammered.

Although she'd seen many criminal cases during her years on the force, she hadn't expected an eerie site in her B&B.

"I'm awfully sorry if I startled you," she apologized.

Soon enough, everyone was upstairs, crowding behind Diana and the mysterious mess on the ground.

"Shall we call the police?" Elliot suggested.

"I think so," Diana replied. "It's probably just a practical joke, but it's best if we report it. I'll get Bobby to come sort this mess out," Diana sighed. "Please get back to your dinner, everyone. I'm so sorry to have disrupted your meal."

The guests returned to the dining hall and resumed enjoying the delicious spread.

Diana hoped this wouldn't affect her business. She'd only been open for several weeks and had put her heart and soul into earning a sterling reputation. She busied herself, removing dirty plates and cups from the various tables.

Suddenly, Elliot stood up. "I'm just going to say it," He announced. "Amy was poking around the mine and went to bother Old Smithy's family. His ghost is obviously unhappy and has come to give us a warning."

"Oh, that's silly!" Diana laughed, brushing off the talk of ghosts.

"What kind of warning?" asked Amy. "It's not like I dug up a treasure or opened a tomb or something!"

Mr. Johnson interjected, "He's right."

Diana gasped. "It's probably a warning to let sleeping dogs lie. Let the old miner and his secrets rest easy." She placed the dishes down and asserted, "This is just a silly old legend, everyone."

The room fell silent as everyone turned to look at her.

She took a deep breath and continued, "The story of the miner has nothing to do with what happened here tonight. What we experienced was either an ugly prank or an attempted burglary." She sighed.

Diana kept her composure and smiled. She was used to taking charge and was a natural leader. "There are no ghosts, Elliot," she finished.

Everyone returned to eating dinner and soon started on dessert.

As her guests retired to their rooms, Diana cleared the dining room and prepared it for the next morning. She returned to the kitchen to help Bobby with the dishes.

There she noticed that her K9 rescue dogs were salivating at the leftovers on the counter.

"I reckon you two deserve a spoil," Diana cooed sweetly while rubbing their heads. "Bobby, be a dear and cut them each a chunky piece of lamb, will you?"

"Sure, Miss D.," Bobby replied.

"Thank you, Bobby," said Diana, grateful for the help.

Bobby cut the meat and dished large portions into the dogs' bowls.

Rover, the younger pup, ravaged his decadent treat and looked up at Diana with hungry eyes.

She laughed. "Aren't you an absolute glutton? Fine, Rover, I'll get you another portion.

Sparky was slightly older, and she seemed to savor her meal. Every bite seemed deliberate, as if she was trying to make the moment last.

"Should I add a few slivers of lamb to Peaches and Mittens bowls as well?" Bobby asked as he finished cutting all the meat.

"Hmmmm," Diana pondered. "Perhaps some of the chicken. They might enjoy something tender and juicy."

Bobby nodded.

"Come to think of it, Bobby, I haven't seen Mittens since last night. She crept in awfully late, and when I woke up, she was already gone."

"That's odd. She usually sits on the back porch all afternoon," Bobby answered.

The pair finished packing away the dishes, and Bobby went home.

Diana made her way upstairs and took another look at the spot where she found the footprints earlier.

I wonder what this was all about. Why did the tracks stop in the middle of the lobby without a trace? Her mind raced with many questions about the odd occurrence.

Rover and Sparky followed her upstairs. Their warm bodies snuggled up to her, making her feel safe.

"Goodnight, my rascals," Diana whispered lovingly as she closed her eyes.

Giving into her need to rest, she fell asleep, but even in her slumber, it bothered her that she hadn't seen Mittens all day.

The alarm clock next to Diana's bed displayed bright red digits reading 02:17. Her eyes shot open, and she couldn't seem to shake the feeling of angst that hurled itself around in the pit of her belly.

She bolted upright, panting and sweating as if she'd had a nightmare that she couldn't remember. Despite the hour, she swung her legs over the side of the bed and slipped her feet into her blue satin slippers.

She then donned her robe and trotted downstairs to make herself a cup of tea. She was fiercely worried about Mittens. In the kitchen, she took out a few of the chocolate chip cookies she'd baked for breakfast.

She then took her midnight snack to the dining room to enjoy. Diana loved dipping her cookies in the tea to watch how they melted. It was a strange habit that she picked up from her grandmother, Hannah.

She relished the memories of their time together when she was a child. The B&B was once Hannah's home, and when she passed away, Diana inherited it.

It made sense since she was Hannah's only remaining relative.

Diana fondly recalled how she and her grandmother had pretended to be private investigators and how those games inspired her to join the force. She also remembered her grandmother's rendition of the Old Smithy tale.

"It's not as deep a mystery as the town's people suspect," her grandmother would utter. "If someone wants the truth, they'll find it. But, if someone is looking to find the treasure to get rich, they'll miss the answers that are right in front of them."

Diana smiled at the memories. Her thoughts were soon interrupted by the sound of creaking footsteps coming down the stairs. She was alert and stood up from the table quietly, ready to catch the burglar or prankster in the act.

She snuck behind a pillar to hide from view and carefully peered around the side to catch a glimpse of the culprit.

The sound stopped, and the retired detective could see a slender silhouette. The figure drew closer. The retired detective took a deep breath, and as she prepared to attack the mysterious figure, Amy came into full view.

"Diana? What are you doing?" Amy asked, surprised, noticing her odd behavior.

"I could ask you the same question," Diana replied curiously.

Then, regaining her composure, realized how silly she must have looked.

She sighed. "I came down for a cup of tea and some cookies; care to join me?"

Amy's concerned expression broke into a smile. "I'd love to. I'm a bit of a night owl, and I heard noises. I came down to convince myself that I was being paranoid after the incident at dinner."

Diana giggled. "Let's not tell the others how silly we've been. I'll get you a cup of tea."

Chapter 3

Amy was quite talkative and explained to Diana that she'd come to the Midwest to get over a particularly difficult relationship. She needed time just to think and get away from everything.

"I didn't think the miner mystery would intrigue me this much," she confessed. "But it's really helping me keep my mind off Jake."

Diana nodded sympathetically. "I know it's a really random way to get over a tumultuous relationship, but for some reason, it's working for me. I'll admit what happened tonight has me spooked a bit. Do you think it was his ghost?"

Her eyes were large with worry. The earnest expression made Diana chortle with surprise.

"Sorry, Love, but there are no ghosts. Even if someone wants us to believe there are."

Amy insisted on helping Diana clear away their dishes, then headed upstairs. Diana followed a few paces behind and noticed that, once again, the upper lobby window was open.

"Did you open the window when you came down?" Diana inquired curiously.

Amy shook her head. She seemed frightened to proceed.

"Well, clearly, the ghost believes we need more ventilation," Diana joked as she closed the window.

"Goodnight, Amy. I'll have a repairman look at the window in the morning," Diana winked and headed to her room.

The old detective was tired, and she'd have to be up in a few short hours to prepare breakfast. Most days, she liked putting her heart and soul into her meals, but she considered keeping it simple this time.

She closed her eyes, and it felt like barely five minutes had passed when her 6 a.m. alarm went off. She greeted Sparky and Rover, then pulled her bed straight.

After she took a hot shower and got dressed, she darted to the kitchen to put together something simple yet scrumptious.

She decided on a frittata with fresh spinach, tomatoes, green and yellow peppers topped off with melted cheese. The coffee maker whirred as it brewed a particularly strong blend of Brazilian grounds.

Diana also put together a batch of pancakes and waffles with an array of syrups. Breakfast was a little later than usual.

She found the guests waiting in the dining area by the time she was ready to serve it all. She glanced at her watch, 8:05. It was strange that Bobby hadn't arrived yet.

She tended to her guests by herself when the phone rang. She tried to answer, but the caller hung up before she could say a word.

"Excuse me for a moment," Diana announced to the guests as she vanished into the kitchen.

She called the number back.

"Miss D? Hello," Bobby's voice came from the other end of the line.

"Bobby, where are you? Why did you call me from a strange number?" she questioned.

"I'm calling from the doctor's office. I'm sorry, I won't be able to come in today; I'm not feeling well."

"Oh no, Bobby. I hope you feel better soon. Don't worry about the B&B; I'll manage," Diana tried to sound upbeat despite not getting enough sleep last night.

She took a deep breath and wiped the sweat from her brow. Then, she returned to the dining hall.

"Apologies, everyone," Diana announced. "My assistant Bobby won't be in today, and I might be a bit slow catering to you all, so please bear with me. I'll do my best to ensure no one gets cold coffee, but no promises today."

Diana smiled kindly, keeping her demeanor light-hearted and hospitable. She moved from table to table, refilling orange juice and coffee.

Once it seemed like everyone had finished, she started clearing the tables. Amy stood up and started helping.

"No, no, no, Dear," Diana scolded while trying to take a few dirty plates from Amy's hands. "You're my guest; no need for all that."

Amy shook her head and responded, "Be that as it may, on the first day, you said to make myself at home, and this is how I do that."

Diana giggled. "It's not necessary, Amy, really."

"I insist," she replied. "If you want space in the kitchen, I can respect that. But I'll help you clear this mess and take the dogs on their morning walk."

Diana relented and smiled, "I appreciate that, Amy."

Most of the guests left the B&B almost immediately after breakfast, except Mr. Franklin. He sat quietly reading the newspaper on a sofa near the entrance.

Diana washed the dishes and skimmed through some recipe books for lunch ideas. She'd do her best to get everything done by herself today.

The incident with the prints and Mitten's disappearance also played on her mind.

As she headed upstairs to fetch fresh tablecloths, Mr. Franklin stopped her.

"Diana," he called softly. "Have you got a moment?"

She stopped, smiled, and nodded. "Certainly. How can I help?"

The old detective did her best to hide her flustered state.

"I'd like to extend my stay," said Mr. Franklin.

"That's wonderful, Mr. Franklin," Diana answered. "I'm not expecting any other guests for a week, so you are more than welcome."

Diana wondered why she'd said that last bit.

Mr. Franklin nodded, and Diana proceeded up the stairs. She was glad the odd occurrences weren't having an effect on her business and felt relieved that one of her guests wanted to stay longer.

In the upstairs lobby, she found that the painting was crooked once again and straightened it on her way to the linen closet. Her phone buzzed in her pocket.

DING! DING! DING!

Multiple text messages flooded the device. The first was from Amy.

Amy: Hi Diana, I wanted to know if I could stay a couple of days extra? I need more time away, and my boss has approved my leave for another week.

"How odd," Diana muttered out loud.

"What is?" asked Mr. Johnson, who had just come out of his room.

"Sorry, Mr. Johnson," Diana blushed. "I was just talking to myself. I thought you and Mrs. Johnson were going on the mine tour this morning?"

"We did. We came back." He croaked. "What did you find so odd? Did you find something else suspicious? Perhaps a clue to the culprit who has us all on edge?" He questioned curiously.

Diana shook her head.

"No matter," Mr. Johnson shrugged. "By the way, I've been meaning to ask you, do you have availability for four more days? Grace simply loves your cooking and was wondering if we might celebrate our 40th anniversary here instead of back home."

What is going on? Diana thought. *How strange that so many guests need to extend their stay.* But she was glad, nonetheless.

" Yes, of course," she stammered. "It should be fine." She mustered a polite smile.

"Fantastic," he replied as he headed back into his room.

Diana checked the rest of her text messages. The second one was from Miriam.

Miriam: Hi Di, how is everything? Just checking in to see how you're doing and if your nostalgia for sleuthing has settled.

Diana smirked as she replied to Miriam.

Diana: You won't believe the weird things that have been happening here. First, there were odd muddy footprints that stopped in the middle of the lobby and vanished. Windows seem to open themselves lately, and my guests are all asking questions about Old Smithy.

After resetting the dining area, Diana finally had a minute to herself. She made a cup of tea and sat in the back garden by the pool.

She had barely started relaxing when Rover came barking along and pounced on top of her, licking her face. Diana howled with laughter as she rubbed his head.

"I missed you too, boy," she said playfully.

Sparky and Amy appeared moments later.

"Thank you so much, Amy," Diana sighed. "They would have been so disappointed to have forfeited their morning walk."

"No worries," Amy beamed. "Also, you haven't replied to my text."

"Oops. I'm such a scatterbrain today. Yes, of course, you can stay longer," Diana assured her.

"Awesome! By the way, since everyone is blaming me for the whole restless ghost thing, I'm going to take another look at the mine. Do you want to join me?" offered Amy.

Diana really didn't feel like it but didn't want to seem rude.

"That's so kind of you, Amy, but I've got my hands full here," Diana replied.

"Nonsense, we have a couple of hours before lunchtime, and we won't be long. Besides, don't you want to get to the bottom of the mysterious footprints?" Amy begged.

Diana sighed. "Fine, let me get my things."

The pair took a short stroll to the mine. It was a pleasant day with blue skies and only a few wispy clouds. There was a cool eastern breeze that lowered the intensity of the heat.

At the mine entrance, the tour operator was nowhere to be found. Amy and Diana waited for ten minutes.

"Let's go in by ourselves," Amy suggested. "He's probably on an early lunch."

Diana hesitated, but Amy pulled her gently by the arm.

"Come on, Diana," she insisted.

The entrance was well-lit, but after five minutes of walking, it got darker. Amy whipped out a flashlight from her handbag.

"This is the way we took the last time," she announced, pointing to a cave on the left. "The guide told us that the two on the right get too narrow as you proceed and have been declared unsafe for more than half a century."

Diana nodded. She wasn't even sure what she was doing here. *Am I looking for a ghost?* She giggled softly at the thought.

"What's up?" Amy asked with a furrowed brow, interrupting Diana's thoughts.

"I was just imagining getting stuck in the narrow part of the cave, getting chased by Old Smithy's ghost in a cocopan..."

"Yeah, like in the cartoons!" Amy added with a chuckle.

As they turned a corner, they saw a male figure ahead of them. He was gently poking at the rubble on the wall.

The duo gasped in shock, and Amy shone her light directly at the man. He was covered in dirt. They backed up slightly as the figure started turning around.

"We come in peace Old Smithy!" Amy called unexpectedly before she could see his face. Fear and excitement were pulsating through her veins.

Diana, who was more level-headed, burst out laughing. "Amy, that's not a ghost! It's Elliot."

"Get the light out of my face Amy," he said brusquely. "Did you seriously think I was a ghost?"

Amy giggled. "Sorry, Elliot, your presence was unexpected. What are you doing here anyway?" She asked, gripping her flashlight tightly.

"Same as yo—"

"OOII!!" A loud voice boomed from behind them, interrupting Elliot and startling Amy once again.

"No one's permitted in here without a tour operator," the voice scolded. "It's a safety risk! Please, everyone out."

The trio made their way back toward the entrance.

"Nobody has been in those caverns for more than 50 years. They were closed off and declared unsafe by Old Smithy himself," said the guide as they walked along.

Amy and Diana exchanged glances.

"He was checking the safety of one of the caverns when it collapsed. Back then, there was no equipment to safely retrieve his body. That's why they say the mine is haunted." The guide continued without being prompted.

"After he died, it wasn't even a few months until the place was shut down. Hundreds of good men lost their income. It's not a place for city slickers to go prancing around," he finished, his eyes fixated on Amy.

"Hey, I remember you. You came here a couple of days ago sniffing for information about Old Smithy." the guide muttered.

Amy pursed her lips.

"Sorry for the trouble," Diana commented, taking the focus off her guest. "We'll be leaving now."

She then took out a small wad of cash and handed it to the guide. "We never got to pay the entrance fee before, as there was no one at the post."

His eyes grew wide at the realization that the group might report him.

"We all have little mishaps," Diana winked as she walked past him.

The three made their way back to the B&B.

Chapter 4

Diana washed up and then prepared lunch. She was glad that Amy dragged her along to explore the mine but knew that she didn't have much time, so she opted for a quick yet hearty meal.

She prepared a mini quinoa bowl for each guest to get their appetites going. It contained a variety of flavorful fillings like avocado, cherry tomatoes, grilled chicken, and black beans.

She also prepared roasted sweet potatoes, corn on the cob, and a Greek salad. The main course was a particularly large salmon seasoned to perfection.

"Something's missing, Peaches," Diana pondered out loud to her cooking companion.

As soon as the words left her lips, her heart sank. She was referring to the food, but the realization of Mittens going missing caused a pang of concern.

She loved all her pets, and their presence brightened her days.

"Garlic bread!" She finally announced. "And a couple of chocolate chip cookies for something sweet."

Diana carefully prepared and kneaded the dough while her mind remained aflutter.

She glanced at all the dishes she had to do and decided to tackle as many as possible while the bread baked.

As soon as the bread was done, lunch was served. Diana felt relieved that everything was ready on time. It gave her great pleasure to watch her guests savor the meal.

She put a jar of fruit punch on each table and politely asked everyone to help themselves.

Amy's green eyes caught Diana's. She made an inconspicuous gesture for Diana to go to the kitchen.

The retired detective obeyed the cue, and Amy quietly followed.

"Diana, you're looking a little weary. Why don't you take a bit of a break, and I'll clear the tables when everyone is done."

Grateful for the concern, Diana smiled. "Amy, you've done more than enough, I couldn't possibly expect more help."

"Ok, then just disappear for ten minutes to get yourself together... a breather as you will," Amy persisted.

Diana sighed. "I must really be getting old if my guests want me to rest," she teased. "Thank you, Amy. I'll just freshen up and be back to clear everything."

Amy beamed.

Diana discreetly made her way upstairs. Most of her guests hadn't noticed, but Elliot eyed her from his table in the corner.

He ate alone, with his laptop open.

Once in the upstairs lobby, Diana saw more footprints. This time the shoe size was much smaller. It started at the window and ended in the middle of the lobby.

She quickly got out the vacuum and cleaned it up. The last thing she wanted to do was cause further alarm. She then straightened the crooked painting and returned to her room for a few moments' rest.

She texted Miriam.

Diana: It's been quite the day! Mittens, my kitty, is still missing. My assistant is out sick. Send help! A superhero squad would be ideal—especially if they could do the dishes.

She ended off her text with a funny face to imply that she was just being silly.

Moments later, her phone rang.

"Hi, Miriam."

"Diana, are you okay? Do you need help at the B&B? I can take some time off?" Miriam offered.

"No, no, I'm fine. It's just a lack of sleep, I guess. I found more prints this afternoon, and I took a visit to the mine caverns. Apparently, Old Smithy declared certain passages in that place unsafe," Diana explained.

"For someone who's been gone half for half a decade, he sure is giving you a hard time," Miriam replied.

"Ha! You don't know half of it!" Diana laughed.

Talking to Miriam always lifted her spirits.

Her friend's tone softened. "I'm worried about you, Di. I'll come over on Sunday and maybe spend a couple of nights there."

"Absolutely not. You'll keep me out of work, and nothing will get done!" Diana joked.

"Well, all work and no play makes a dull retired detective," Miriam sassed.

"I can't wait to see you, my friend. I'll prepare an incredible feast with all your favorites. Let me get back to my chores."

After her call with Miriam, Diana felt invigorated. She marched downstairs and cleaned up.

Her thoughts were still unsettled. *Why was Elliot alone in the cave that day? What was he doing poking at the rocks, and how long had he been in there before they arrived?*

Elliot had been suspiciously quiet since their experience at the mine. He chose the most isolated table and covered his laptop whenever someone passed by.

Diana had just finished the dishes when a text arrived.

DING!

Miriam: Di, I've been thinking about your situation. Maybe it's time to do some digging. Didn't you always tell me that your grandmother said the mystery could be solved? P.S., looking forward to some sweet potato pie (hint).

Diana giggled.

Peaches walked up to her and pounced right into her arms.

"Aww, my sweetheart. This cuddle is so needed right now."

She walked toward the window and sat on the nearby chair while stroking Peaches' soft fur.

The rest of the day seemed to buzz by in a blur. Without Bobby around, Diana was beginning to truly feel like a woman in her mid-fifties. All the bustling about, cleaning, and taking care of her guests left her feeling slightly out of breath by the time dinner rolled around.

She still managed to prepare a delectable supper. The spread included roasted turkey with gravy, buttery mashed potatoes, and honey-glazed carrots. There was also a green bean casserole, apple walnut salad, and cranberry sauce.

She kept the dessert simple, with mixed berry trifle and a chocolate pecan pie.

She barely managed to socialize with her guests as she hurried back and forth between the kitchen and dining area.

Once again, Amy came to the rescue and offered to help her with the dishes. The pair finished cleaning at around 10 p.m. and headed straight to bed. Diana was grateful for Amy's help and decided to give her one night's free stay.

She was appreciative that no weird things were happening. She just wanted to get into her cozy queen size bed and dive into dreamland.

Diana rose bright and early on Thursday morning. She whipped up a batch of pancakes and blueberry muffins. She also fried some sausages and made her own hash browns.

"Good morning, Peaches," she chimed cheerfully as her tabby cat made her way to her usual sunny spot. It was a particularly warm morning, so the retired detective decided on a refreshing fruit salad and yogurt parfait to accompany her baked goods.

Mr. Franklin didn't attend breakfast, which seemed odd as he was usually an early riser.

"Ooh, Diana, can I have this muffin recipe?" Mrs. Johnson asked as she tucked into her third one.

Diana smiled. "Certainly. It was one of my grandmother's favorite recipes."

Mrs. Johnson nodded as she indulged in the decadent treat. "Was she from around here?"

"Yes," Diana answered politely. "In fact, this was her house."

Mrs. Johnson's facial expression changed. "Did she know anything about the miner legend?"

"I can't be sure," Diana replied quickly and made her way to another table.

After breakfast, Bobby arrived. He brought some fresh flowers for the dining area and took Sparky and Rover on their morning walk.

She was so glad to have her assistant back. Diana tidied up upstairs. She changed sheets, replaced towels, and filled toiletries. It seemed that she could hear soft meowing all over the B&B.

"Where could that noise be coming from?" she whispered to herself as she made her way back downstairs.

Elliot sat in the furthest corner of the dining area. He was typing furiously on his laptop.

"Is everything okay, Elliot?" Diana inquired kindly.

He jolted upright, almost startled, and slammed his laptop shut. "I'll finish up the rest of this in my room," he said nervously.

"Oh my. I didn't mean to give you a fri..." Diana spoke, but he had raced up the stairs before she could finish her sentence.

She pondered how odd that was. Her suspicions suddenly fell to Elliot. *He had left the dining area to go wash up when the prints occurred. What was he doing at the mine? Why was he suddenly abrupt?*

Diana's mind was ablaze. Suddenly the sleuth in her mind had been awakened.

Later that afternoon, when Elliot stepped out, she cleaned his room and checked his shoe size. She wanted to know if it matched that of the intruder who left the prints.

It was size 11, a bit too small to match the first set, which was roughly a size 13, and too big to match the second set, which looked like a lady's size seven.

Disappointed, Diana exited Elliot's room. As she did, she found Mrs. Johnson in the lobby, staring curiously at her.

"Just filled up the toilet paper in here," she smiled, trying to act natural.

"Ours needs filling, too," Mrs. Johnson added.

Diana nodded and got her a few rolls from the cupboard. Then, she headed to the kitchen to cook dinner.

After glancing through her massive recipe book, she opted for macaroni and cheese with garlic-roasted broccoli and crispy baked chicken. She paired it with an aromatic pumpkin pie and sugary apple crisp dessert.

While she prepared the chicken, Elliot entered the kitchen.

"Diana, about earlier," he swallowed hard.

The B&B owner turned away from the counter to look at him.

"I'm sorry I snapped at you. I guess I was just feeling guilty," he continued.

Diana's stomach churned. Were her suspicions correct?

"I've been sent here by my family's hotel group to see if it's safe to open a holiday resort here. You've been so kind to me, and I know it's going to impact your business negatively if we do."

The retired detective remained silent.

"The other day, at the mine, I was collecting samples for the lab to make sure there were no harmful chemicals that could cause us a loss. A couple of years ago, we lost millions in a mining town that had asbestos residue."

"Why are you confessing all this to me?" Diana inquired.

"I figured the least I could do was be honest with you. You don't deserve to be blindsided," he confessed.

"Have you been causing the prints? To sabotage me before you start building?" she asked worriedly.

"No, not at all," he asserted. "All I did was scout the area... and the competition."

Diana nodded and smiled as she gained her composure and slid a stray black hair behind her ear. "I appreciate your honesty, Elliot."

Then she turned back to her dinner prep. Tears filled her hazel eyes. She was a tough cookie, but this B&B was sentimental to her.

When dinner was almost ready, Diana popped upstairs to freshen up before serving. She washed her hands and face and reapplied her makeup.

"You'll be okay, old girl," she spoke to her reflection. "No big hotel group can match your hospitality."

She plastered on a smile and entered the upstairs lobby. Right beneath the crooked painting sat a sight for sore eyes.

"Mittens!" Diana exclaimed happily as she rushed toward her pet.

The cat had a ball of bright yellow yarn and was playing cheerfully.

"Oh, I have missed you. I'm so glad you're okay!"

She scooped the cat into her arms and held her tight.

"My goodness, Mittens, where have you been? Your fur is incredibly dusty."

Chapter 5

Preparing breakfast was an absolute joy now that Diana had the company of both her cats again. She prepared sausages, bacon, eggs, and waffles with maple syrup. She hummed as she worked.

"Good morning Amy," she beamed as her first guest sat down to eat.

"Good morning. You seem to be in a good mood," Amy answered.

"Yes!" Diana explained. "My Mittens is back! I was so worried that she was stuck in the mine."

"I'm glad for you, Diana. Where did you find her?"

"The upstairs lobby," Diana replied as she started serving the rest of the guests.

"Is she okay? Hurt in any way?" Amy asked, concerned.

"She seemed fine to me, but I'll take her to the vet a bit later just to be sure."

Amy nodded. "How long have you had her?"

"Only a couple of weeks. They had just found her when I got to the pet shelter. I had already had Peaches and the pups for a couple of months, and I just fell in love with her there and then," Diana recalled.

"Aww, that's so sweet, Diana."

"Yeah, I'm just glad she's safe."

Amy frowned and said, "Don't you find it strange that *everything* keeps happening in that lobby."

Diana stopped in her tracks.

Amy raised her eyebrows to emphasize her point, then turned her gaze to her meal. She then enjoyed her breakfast with great enthusiasm.

Diana left the dishes to Bobby and decided to inspect the upstairs lobby carefully. Mittens was enjoying a nap on the thick windowsill where the sun's golden rays poured in.

She checked the ceiling and the walls, but nothing stood out to her. Then, she disturbed her resting cat to inspect the window. All was in order.

She felt perplexed. The seasoned sleuth thought hard for a moment and looked at the painting of two young sweethearts holding hands on the beach.

"Why does this painting always go crooked by itself, Mittens?" she pondered.

Suddenly her eyes fell to the ground, to the spot where the floor meets the wall. The long rug seemed to have somehow jammed beneath the wall, but how was that possible?

Diana tugged and tugged at it, but it was stuck—almost as if the wall was built on top of it. It intrigued her.

She began searching along the wall for clues as to how this happened. She straightened the painting. She pressed hard against the bricks and tried looking for oddities but to no avail.

After Elliot's confession, Diana had an inkling that he had something to do with this. Business sabotage in the most creative way. But how did he manage to get the carpet under the wall?

"We'll be keeping a close eye on 'Mr. Holiday Resort,' won't we, Mittens?" Diana inquired.

She glanced at her watch. It was a dainty silver Michel Herbelin, one of the first ever produced back in 1952—Another sentimental inheritance from her grandmother.

"Good grief, Mittens! Look at the time! I have to get the shopping done before lunch!"

Diana hurriedly grabbed her purse and headed downstairs. She needed a variety of ingredients. Among them were fresh fruits and vegetables.

As she passed the dining area, she noticed Elliot was still glued to the same spot he'd been in during breakfast. His eyes were fixated on his screen, and his demeanor was tense.

Careful not to startle him, Diana cleared her throat. He looked up at her.

Diana smiled kindly. "Would you like something to drink while you work? There's lemonade in the fridge."

He reciprocated with a grateful smile. "That would be wonderful, thank you."

She popped into the kitchen. Bobby was just wrapping up the morning's dishes when she arrived.

Diana filled a jar with ice cubes and lemonade. She proceeded to gently place a slice of lemon on the side of a glass and placed it all on a tray.

"Miss D, could I pop out for a bit? We're running low on dog food." Bobby asked.

"Ah, I'm on my way to the produce market now, but I'll add it to my list for the grocery store," she replied cheerily.

Bobby looked dismayed.

Diana realized that he might have wanted to run a personal errand as well.

"Tell you what, Bobby," she said, "it's such a hot day, and I don't really feel like walking in this heat. Maybe you could do the shopping for me when you get the dog food? I have a list."

Bobby grinned. "Of course! It won't take more than an hour."

Diana handed him the list and took the lemonade to Elliot. He seemed to be preoccupied with something.

"This is perfect! Thank you, Diana," Elliot exclaimed as he poured himself a glass.

"Is there anything else I can help with?"

Elliot shook his head. "Just work stuff. I'll stay here until lunch if that's okay. There's less chance of me procrastinating if I'm here."

Diana nodded and headed upstairs to fetch her phone. She wanted to text Miriam about her suspicions.

As she reached the lobby, she noticed muddy prints on the carpet again. Size 13 prints. They started in the middle of the lobby and ended at the window.

The rug was also no longer stuck beneath the wall, and the painting of the lovers was crooked once again. The old detective sighed in bewilderment.

Diana fetched the vacuum and tried to remove all evidence of an intruder. She felt flustered. Her top suspect hadn't moved from the dining area all day. His shoes were neat and clean, and she hadn't been in the kitchen long enough for him to stage this prank.

Some of the prints left stains, so she made a mixture of laundry detergent and warm water. She then got on her hands and knees to scrub them away.

The chore reminded her of when she was younger, and her grandmother would turn carpet cleaning into a game.

She recalled her granny's words. "You scrub that half, and I'll scrub this half, and we'll meet in the middle."

Whenever they finished a room, her grandmother would bake a treat to celebrate a job well done. Diana felt joy at the resurgence of such a simple yet special memory.

Soon all traces of mud were gone. She emptied the bucket and finally texted Miriam.

Diana: Hi, Miriam. Good news! Mittens came home! I can't wait to see you. There is just so much going on. It's been such a crazy day! Every time I think I've got this whole mystery figured out; it turns out I'm wrong.

Soon, Bobby returned, and Diana started lunch.

The kitchen was warm, and an array of enticing aromas emanated from the room.

She baked ciabatta bread for caprese sandwiches, which she assembled with fresh basil, ripe tomatoes, and mozzarella cheese. The final step was drizzling them with a delectable glaze.

In the oven were spinach and feta stuffed chicken breasts and roasted potatoes.

While the main course baked, she chopped an assortment of vegetables, including zucchini and bell peppers. These would complement her pasta primavera perfectly.

To end lunch on a sweet note, Diana prepared a classic, sweet cherry pie. She made her filling from scratch with a sugary jam base that gave off an irresistible scent.

As Diana cooked, she felt all her worries dissipate. She was in the zone, relaxed, and pouring her heart into each dish.

"Another beautiful meal is ready," she boasted to herself cheekily as she took the cherry pie out of the oven.

Bobby served lunch, and she poured herself a glass of lemonade. Diana wondered if Miriam had responded and checked her pocket for her phone.

"Oh, Peaches, I'm such a scatterbrain. I'm going to have massive leg muscles soon from running up and down the stairs all day for my phone," she giggled.

Diana made her way upstairs again, and when she saw the crooked painting, she felt a pang of worry.

"I'm done straightening this silly painting," she announced to herself and used both arms to remove it from the wall.

It was heavier than she'd anticipated, and she struggled to keep her balance under its weight. She placed it on the ground and noticed a strange indentation in the wall. It was about 2 inches long and in the shape of a small shovel.

She ran her fingers along the hole and felt that it was quite deep. Then

Diana noticed a word written at the back of the painting.

It appeared that the letters were written with a muddy finger. The same color mud as the prints. In the center, it read ATTIC.

Diana inhaled sharply. These were massive clues!

Not wanting to draw suspicion, she put the painting back up. It wasn't an easy feat, but eventually she managed.

She hadn't been up in the attic in years. In fact, many of her parents' and grandparents' belongings were still up there, collecting cobwebs and dust. She wasn't even sure if the light up there still worked.

She thought long and hard. *What if it's a trap? What if someone wants to hurt me in the dark unsuspecting attic? Am I being silly?*

Diana took a deep breath to maintain her composure and fetched her revolver from the safe in her bedroom. It's been a while since she'd felt the need for added protection. She also took a flashlight in case it was completely dark.

She caught a glimpse of herself in the mirror.

"Time to get to the bottom of this old girl," she reassured herself and cautiously made her way to the attic.

The light still worked, but it was extremely dim.

She shone her flashlight around the room while gripping her gun tightly. It seemed safe enough. It was clear that the room had become a sanctuary for spiders and dust mites. A thick layer of dust covered everything, and cobwebs had taken over.

The ambiance was eerie and uncomfortable, even for someone who specialized in sleuthing. She scanned the room for anything out of the ordinary.

Some of the boxes housed toys from her childhood, memorabilia from her early career, and even her father's old football gear.

It was like a dusty trip down memory lane. She'd had a great life. Her family was amazing, and she missed them dearly.

Suddenly a small wooden box near the door caught her eye.

She'd never seen it before, and she knew about everything stored up in the attic. She shone her flashlight on it and gasped.

"Why isn't this covered in dust?" she whispered to herself nervously.

She opened it and realized that it was a beautiful mahogany jewelry box. The design was quite unusual, and it had various compartments inside. Each one had a miniature drawer to open, and they all had a pink velvet base.

Diana opened each little drawer, hoping for the next clue in her investigation. In the last one, she found something and reached in to remove it.

It was a necklace. Nine-carat gold, with a thick clasp. But the most fascinating thing about it was the main embellishment. The pendant was a stunning golden shovel, two inches long. It was also engraved and read: Hannah Smith.

Diana was confused. She had so many questions.

How odd. My grandmother's maiden name was Banner, and her married surname was Fisher. Why would this pendant say Smith? This shovel looks like the perfect fit for the indentation in the lobby wall.

Diana felt a tingling sensation on her forearm. She'd worn short sleeves due to the hot temperatures. As soon as she caught sight of the spider, she stood up, shook it off, and shoved the necklace into her pocket.

"I think I'm about done up here," she whispered. "This investigation just got interesting."

Chapter 6

Diana felt the adrenaline rush she longed for. It was a common sensation when she was on the force, but she had missed it these last couple of months. She shut the attic door and hurried to her room. She wanted to take a warm, soothing shower after being in a dust-filled environment.

She removed the necklace from her pocket and took a closer look at the pendant. There was a series of small oddly shaped cubes at the back of the mini shovel.

How fascinating! she thought.

KNOCK! KNOCK! KNOCK!

The sound of three rapid, firm knocks broke her thoughts. She opened the door, and there stood Mrs. Johnson.

"Hi, Dearie. I'm sorry to be a bother," the elderly lady greeted.

"Mrs. Johnson, hi. It's no bother at all. Is something wrong?" Diana replied, trying to act natural.

"Well, no, I've come to ask a favor…" her words broke as she noticed the gold necklace Diana was holding. "What's that sparkly jewel you have there?" she asked excitedly.

"Oh, this?" responded Diana. "Just an old heirloom." She quickly placed it on her dressing table, which was right by the door. "Tell me about this favor." She smiled, clasping her hands together.

"Well, I'm sure Norman has told you that I wanted to extend our stay to spend our anniversary here."

"Yes! He mentioned that."

"Well, it's our 40th anniversary tomorrow, so I was wondering if you could do something special to celebrate? Decorations, a special menu, things like that?" Mrs. Johnson requested.

The request caught Diana off guard. She'd never hosted an event before. The timing was also a bit challenging, with all the strange happenings. She opened her mouth to respond but closed it again when she saw how hope and excitement glistened in Mrs. Johnson's eyes.

The retired detective inhaled deeply and smiled.

"Of course! It's a major occasion!" Diana exclaimed, matching her guest's excitement. "We'll decorate and create a spectacular setting."

"Oh, Diana, thank you!" Mrs. Johnson responded excitedly.

"If you'd like, we can make arrangements for you to invite a few people," Diana suggested.

"Oh, that would be fantastic. Let's iron out the details after mealtime. It's short notice, so I don't want to put you out of your way."

Diana smiled. "No worries at all, Mrs. Johnson. You can have the event exactly as you like. By the way, where is Mr. Johnson?"

"He's out getting a new suit; of course, I told him I wanted our 40th anniversary to be the most incredible one yet, with lots of photographs," Mrs. Johnson explained. "I got myself a dress, too," she added. Her eyes glistened with youthful exuberance despite her age.

Diana smiled at the sincerity of the lady's love for her husband.

"But anyway, let me not keep you up from your duties, Dearie. We'll talk about this tonight," Mrs. Johnson ended the conversation and ambled to her room.

Diana closed her door and quickly showered. She used the quiet time to reflect on everything going on.

Hannah Smith. It makes no sense. None at all. Was my grandmother married previously? But that doesn't correspond with what I know about her life and her age. Why was the box not dusty? Who had been in the attic? As absurd as this ghost story is, I'm having doubts myself.

Diana allowed her thoughts to run freely as she quickly slipped into a pair of light blue jeans and a navy blue blouse with chiffon frills around the neckline. She then donned a pair of comfortable white shoes and rushed down to the kitchen to start dinner.

Halfway down the stairs, she heard a loud crash of thunder.

"It looks like a storm is coming!" she said aloud while glancing out the windows in the dining area.

Dark gray storm clouds filled the sky, which was sunny only a few hours ago. A powerful wind blew dust and odd bits of litter around, and she could hear things slapping around outside due to its might.

Diana rushed to the kitchen and instructed. "Bobby, please get Sparky and Rover inside."

She examined the kitchen and then added, "See if you can find Mittens and Peaches too. It looks like an unexpected storm is on the way."

"Don't you find it eerie, Miss D? This weather, Old Smithy's prints, the weird guest extensions, and Mittens' disappearance and sudden reappearance," Bobby questioned, his voice seemingly higher than usual, almost as if he was afraid.

Diana turned and looked at him calmly.

"Bobby, please bring the animals inside safely before the downpour starts. And bring in any loose bits and bobs that may fly away with this wind," Diana directed, taking charge of the situation.

Bobby nodded.

The retired detective then diverted her attention to making a warm and filling dinner. The main meal was a hearty, flavorful mutton stew. She accompanied it with freshly baked crusty bread and creamy mashed potatoes. Lastly, she added a simple salad as a palate cleanser.

Guests began settling in the dining area when she realized that she hadn't made anything for dessert.

Sparky and Rover lay next to each other, close to the warmth of the oven, while Peaches and Mittens purred happily on chair cushions. Bobby cleaned the counters after Diana's dinner preparations.

"Bobby! I've forgotten about dessert!" she laughed, returning from the dining area.

Bobby raised an eyebrow.

"It's dinner time, and there's nothing for dessert!" Diana repeated, clearly baffled at her own forgetfulness.

"Miss D, I'm sure you can whip up something in no time," he reassured her as he went back to cleaning.

"Just put together one of those fruity cinnamon things. It's fast and delicious and will be ready before they're done eating," Bobby added, not looking up from his task.

"Ah, Bobby, you're brilliant!" Diana exclaimed with relief as she gave him a quick hug.

Bobby chuckled.

Diana put together a fruit crumble with the fresh produce from the market. Soon the kitchen was filled with aromas of baked apples and peaches sprinkled with cinnamon.

The alluring scent wafted to the dining area, where her guests eagerly awaited the final course of their meal.

When Diana served it, Bobby offered each guest a topping of either whipped cream or ice cream. Everyone chomped away happily.

"Bobby, I haven't had a chance to ask. What did the vet say about Mittens when you took her in earlier?" Diana asked, concerned.

Bobby smiled as he looked over at Mittens.

"Well?"

"Miss D, all is well with Mittens; no worries," Bobby replied. "She's just not eaten as well as she would have if she were home."

"My sweet Mittens, we'll fatten you up in no time," she whispered as she turned to the staircase. "Bobby, I'm turning in early. Please lock up before you leave."

Her assistant nodded.

Upstairs she found Mittens purring loudly. She was scratching the wall.

"Hey, Baby," Diana cooed. "It's okay. I know the storm is scary." She scooped her cat into her arms and gently stroked her fur.

She consoled Mittens with a soothing voice all the way down the lobby until they got to the bedroom.

Once there, Diana brushed her teeth, changed into sweatpants and a white t-shirt, and got into bed. It had been a busy day, and she felt unusually tired.

"A good night's rest will do us both the world of good Mittens. I'll figure out the connection between the necklace and the wall tomorrow," she announced as she pulled up the blanket.

Mittens didn't share her thoughts. Moments later, the cat made her way through the pet door back into the lobby. She continued curiously scratching at the wall.

It didn't take long for Diana to fall asleep. Her dreams were vivid and intense, merging all the events together.

She also dreamed of her father's encouraging eyes, as he had always looked whenever she had told him about the mysteries she'd encountered throughout her career. He was always supportive and kind. As the first rays of sunshine filtered through the curtains, the images in her mind were peaceful and serene.

On Saturday morning, for the first time in a long time, Diana woke up before her alarm. She felt refreshed and ready to discover the connection between the necklace and the indentation on the wall.

It was 6:05 a.m. Most of her guests were likely to still be asleep. It was the ideal time to poke around the lobby undisturbed.

Diana swung her legs off the edge of her bed and stretched. Then, she brushed her teeth, washed up, got dressed, and headed to her dressing table near the door to retrieve the necklace.

When she got there, the necklace was gone. It was replaced by a note. The handwriting was slanted and crafted in capital letters.

I'VE RETURNED TO MY HOME. I'M NOT SAFE JUST LYING AROUND.

Chills ran down Diana's spine. Someone had been in her bedroom while she was asleep!

She felt concerned at the violation of her privacy and even a little scared. What if these occurrences were leading to something dangerous?

At first, she suspected business sabotage, but Elliot was in the dining area when the latest set of prints appeared. Nobody knew she had the necklace.

Diana replayed the previous day's events in her mind.

"Mrs. Johnson?" she gasped out loud.

The retired detective recalled that Mrs. Johnson asked about the necklace when she came to discuss the anniversary dinner. Her suspicions shifted to the elderly couple. Diana considered the facts.

It might also explain why the footprints have different sizes. The larger ones are probably Mr. Johnson, and the smaller ones might belong to his wife.

Diana thought about inspecting their room but changed her mind. As a seasoned sleuth, she knew the truth would come out sooner or later.

She tied her dark shoulder-length hair into a low ponytail and hurried downstairs to make breakfast.

She cooked scrambled eggs, sausages, bacon, and grilled tomatoes. On the side, she prepared a large serving of baked beans and fried mushrooms. The scents were enticing, and Diana believed that a couple of muffins would complement the meal perfectly.

She whipped out her grandmother's recipe book and flipped through the pages.

"Chocolate muffins," she announced to herself.

She carefully measured the ingredients and poured them into her mixing bowl.

"Good morning Miss D," said Bobby as he entered the kitchen.

"Good morning Bobby," she responded cheerfully.

Bobby smiled and looked around to see what needed to be done.

"Be a darling and squeeze the rest of those oranges for me, please," Diana requested.

Bobby immediately got started.

"I came in early because getting everything ready in time for the dinner party tonight may take longer than usual," he added.

"Oh yes! Mr. and Mrs. Johnson's anniversary dinner!" Diana exclaimed.

The occasion had slipped her mind until now. She suddenly remembered that she hadn't spoken to Mrs. Johnson about the event's details.

She served breakfast while Bobby, Sparky, and Rover went on their morning walk.

"Good morning Diana!" Amy chimed cheerily as she made her way to a table.

The retired detective smiled. "Hi, Amy. Have you slept well?"

Amy nodded.

Mr. Franklin and the Johnsons sat together and soon began chatting as they enjoyed the delicious meal.

"Good morning Diana," Mr. Johnson greeted them as the retired detective filled their coffee.

"Morning all," she replied, hiding her suspicion.

"Oh, Dearie, do you think we could have a little chat after breakfast?" Mrs. Johnson asked with a wink.

Diana nodded. "Certainly. I'm so sorry we didn't get around to it yesterday."

Chapter 7

The Johnsons wanted 20 guests to attend their dinner party and told Diana not to mind the expenses involved, especially because it was short notice.

"After this major splurge, we'll spend the rest traveling," Mr. Johnson explained.

Diana made a list of items and asked Bobby to try and purchase them all before lunchtime.

"Bobby, before you leave, do you perhaps have any friends who could assist us with putting this little party together? I have no idea where we'll get some extra hands at this short notice," Diana asked hopefully.

"I sure do," Bobby responded happily.

"Tell them to be here by noon so we can have the party set up and ready by 7 p.m. We still have to serve dinner to the rest of our guests at 8," said Diana.

Bobby nodded and headed out. Diana ran upstairs to send Miriam a text.

Diana: Hi Miriam, hope you're alright. Sorry I haven't texted you until now. There has been so much going on. I found a strange box in the attic and an indentation on my wall. Also, someone managed to sneak into my room last night while I was sleeping, and now my necklace is gone! I'll fill you in on everything when you get here tomorrow. Have a splendid day.

Diana shook her head at how absurd it all sounded.

She diverted her attention to the crisp white note on her dressing table. She pondered over what the words meant.

Then she gasped. "Of course! It's back in the attic!"

She quickly made her way to the attic. She hoped that she could try and figure all of this out before Bobby returned.

The attic door squeaked as she pushed it open. The box was where she had left it.

Diana slowly opened it and found the necklace in the same place as before.

"If I don't figure things out by tomorrow, I'm handing this box over to the police for fingerprints." She whispered to herself as she shut the lid.

Back in the lobby, Amy stood in front of the painting of the two lovers. Diana shoved the necklace into her pocket when she saw her guest.

"Diana, I was actually looking for you," she beamed. "I bumped into Steven, Old Smithy's grandson, at the mall today. He noticed me from my visit."

"Oh my. Did he have anything interesting to say?" the old detective inquired.

"Well, yes. He said we could have a chat tomorrow afternoon about his grandfather and what he knows about the legend," Amy replied.

"So, I invited him to lunch..." her voice trailed off, "here at the B&B." She finished.

Diana smirked. "I see."

"I also told him that you would love to learn more about what the legend says about this building," Amy added, wincing nervously, waiting for Diana's response.

"Amy!" Diana laughed.

The young lady shrugged. "Soon, we'll all have the answers we want. By the way, Bobby said there's going to be a big event in the garden tonight. Mrs. Johnson said to tell you that all your guests are welcome, and you don't have to prepare two separate dinners," Amy responded, changing the subject.

"Well, that certainly makes things easier," Diana smiled.

"Which reminds me, I have to go and get a new outfit. See you later, Diana," Amy called out as she walked toward the stairs.

Once Amy was out of earshot, Diana removed the painting from the wall and carefully placed it flat on the floor. She made sure to leave enough room for her feet so she didn't damage the frame.

She took the necklace out of her pocket and turned it so the shovel end would match the direction of the one on the indentation.

Diana didn't know why, but she was nervous. Her heart's rhythm increased its pace as she moved the pendant toward the wall.

MEEEEOOOOWWWW!

The retired detective drew a sharp, quick breath at the sound and turned her head to look behind her. It was Mittens unexpectedly standing there. It looked as if she was waiting for something.

Diana let out a quiet giggle. She couldn't believe she was startled by her own cat. Then she resumed her mysterious task and placed the pendant against the indentation.

She heard something click. Shortly after, the wall slid toward the left and revealed a dark, dusty secret passage with a spiral staircase. Almost as soon as it opened, Mittens leaped forward and ran at full speed into the darkness.

"Mittens, no! Come back!" Diana called, but her cat was long gone.

Diana noticed there was a lit lantern hanging from a large hook on the right wall. She entered the passage and took the lantern off the hook. As she did, the wall behind her closed.

She took a deep breath and followed the path down the stairs,

"Mittens!" she called. "Come here, girl!"

It was quiet, and the stairs continued for a while before reaching an even surface where the path continued.

The retired detective was sure that she was below ground now. She walked for roughly ten minutes before the path turned sharply to the right.

She could hear Mittens scuffling about.

After another two minutes, she noticed a large arched doorway in the wall on the right, but the path continued past it.

She lifted her lantern to look inside the room. There were no cobwebs, and it had a large red rug in the middle of the floor.

In one corner, there was an antique, two-seater sofa. It looked similar to one her grandmother used to own.

Then she heard meowing.

Cautiously the retired detective entered the hidden room. She lifted the lantern to increase her visibility.

In a corner was a large basket with different colored balls of yarn. There were all kinds of material scraps in there too. As Diana moved closer, she saw them.

"Awww, Mittens. This is where you got that colorful ball of yarn. That's why you were scratching the wall yesterday," Diana spoke softly.

She took a closer look at her surroundings. It was quite cozy, and upon closer inspection, she found a fully stocked bookshelf.

What is this place? Diana wondered.

"Mittens, I think we have to get back to Bakers Inn," Diana whispered.

Cautiously, she made her way back, carrying Mittens. When the pathway ended, she felt around for a way to push the hidden door open. She was unsure how she would be able to get out but knew there must be a way. It was just a matter of figuring out how. She hung the lantern on the hook to get better light, and suddenly the wall opened.

"The weight of the lantern must have triggered the secret door to open!" she marveled in amazement.

Once they were back in the lobby, Diana set Mittens down on the floor and then removed the necklace from the wall and placed it in her pocket.

Within seconds, the secret door slid shut.

She carefully put the painting back and straightened it.

"I've given up on that painting, Miss D," Bobby announced as she walked toward her.

Diana smiled at Bobby. He'd seemed so spooked by everything that had been happening, so she decided to keep her discovery to herself.

"Ah, yes, I know. It always seems to fall crooked after a few hours," she chuckled.

Bobby nodded. "I've actually just come up to tell you that I managed to get all the items on the list."

"Fantastic, Bobby. I'll be down in a little while to prepare lunch and get an early start on dinner."

"Miss D, also, some of the guys are here already... the extra hands you asked for?"

"Wonderful," Diana beamed. "That means you and your friends can start setting up the tables and putting up decorations."

"How do you want it done?" Bobby asked.

Diana enjoyed overseeing everything, but her hands were full today.

"Hmmm. You can see how everything fits best, but leave enough room between the tables and the swimming pool. We don't want any accidents."

"You want me to decide?" Bobby asked, surprised.

Diana nodded confidently. "Of course, Bobby, I trust your judgment."

Bobby grinned at Diana's faith in his abilities.

"I won't let you down, Miss D," he replied as he rushed down the stairs.

Diana had a quick shower to wash off the dust and hurried down to the kitchen to make lunch.

Both Peaches and Mittens lounged around lazily in the patch of sunlight that shone through the kitchen window.

"We have to keep lunch simple. I need to save all my culinary magic for tonight's feast," she said aloud to her pets.

Diana decided on chicken Caesar wraps, chicken noodle soup, stuffed mushrooms, and garlic bread. She worked swiftly and lovingly and prepared everything within an hour.

Bobby served lunch while she started on the colossal task of making an anniversary feast.

Mrs. Johnson had splendid ideas for the event, and Diana was determined to pull it off.

She had everything ready 15 minutes early and was quite pleased.

"Bobby, this is absolutely stunning!" Diana announced as she entered the back garden.

Vibrant navy blue and silver banners fluttered in the breeze. Helium balloons of the same color scheme decorated the garden and were tastefully tied down. Neatly covered seats and tables awaited the guests; each had a centerpiece of fresh flowers.

Bobby and his friends had even transformed the pool into a glistening oasis. Hundreds of flickering candles were floating on its surface.

The buffet was set up in an L-shape, with a two-tiered silver cake on one end. It was surrounded by 100 cupcakes, each adorned with a topper that said 40.

For appetizers, Diana prepared shrimp cocktails, crab cakes, and smoked salmon canapés. Mrs. Johnson wanted a surf and turf menu with mainly seafood options.

The main dishes were seafood paella, pan-seared sea bass, and grilled lobster tails basted with garlic herb butter. On the other side of the table was tender grilled ribeye steak and herb-roasted chicken.

There were also a wide variety of side dishes. These included buttered corn on the cob, grilled asparagus, and Quinoa salad.

When it came to dessert, Diana didn't disappoint. Aside from the eye-catching two-tiered cake and cupcakes, she catered multiple options for those with a sweet tooth.

Guests could indulge in decadent key-lime pie, chocolate-covered strawberries, coconut cream pie, or blueberry parfait.

The retired detective had gone all out. It certainly helped that Mrs. Johnson had allowed her B&B guests to join in on the festivities.

When Mrs. Johnson returned from her trip to the hair salon, Bobby stopped her from going to the back garden.

"Diana insists on it being a surprise," he explained. "We'll get your guests seated, and you and Mr. Johnson can come down together at 7:30 p.m."

Mrs. Johnson agreed excitedly and rushed upstairs to get changed while many of their guests arrived. Bobby and his friends helped to get everyone seated.

Diana put on soft music and got her camera ready as she wanted to record the couple's reaction when they walked in.

Chapter 8

Diana instructed the guests to be as quiet as possible while they waited for the moment to cheer when the couple entered the garden. She pressed the record button on her camera, anticipating their arrival.

Bobby escorted them from the staircase to the curtain of the backyard sliding door. He then pulled back the curtain revealing the spectacular setting, and all the guests stood up and applauded them.

Mr. and Mrs. Johnson's faces lit up with joy. They were grateful for the years spent together and for all those who had come to celebrate this milestone with them. Their hearts swelled with love as they held hands and made their way through the crowd to the table Diana had prepared for them.

"Wow, Diana, this is simply marvelous," Mrs. Johnson exclaimed joyfully.

She sat down at the table and examined the decor. She was appreciative of how Diana paid attention to detail. The setting was flawless.

Bobby and his friends volunteered to be waiters for the event. Everyone chatted and laughed. There were also several heartfelt toasts and speeches made.

Louis, one of Bobby's friends, was a DJ and kept the crowd entertained with familiar tunes.

After eating, Mr. and Mrs. Johnson took to the dance floor. They surprised everyone with how agile they were, and their moves were impressive.

Diana and the guests clapped and cheered as the elderly couple laughed and enjoyed the spotlight.

Many guests soon followed suit, and it was a jovial occasion for all. Diana, Amy, and Elliot took lots of photographs.

By 10 p.m., most of the guests left. Bobby and Diana cleaned up and did as many dishes as they could. They were exhausted from a hard day's work, but the party had brought in a sizable amount of money.

"Bobby, tell your friends they're welcome to a free lunch next weekend, and each of them can bring a plus one. They deserve something special for pulling this all together so quickly and splendidly," Diana said as she scrubbed a pan.

"I'm sure they'd like that very much," Bobby replied.

The pair finished the cleaning just before midnight, and Diana was ready for a good night's sleep.

"Good night Bobby. See you in the morning," Diana yawned as she made her way through the dining area.

She was about to close the sliding door when she saw the Johnsons still sitting outside. They were talking and laughing when Mrs. Johnson saw her standing there.

"Diana, join us," she called cheerfully.

The old detective smiled and walked toward them.

"I didn't mean to interrupt," she replied, "I was just closing up for the night."

"Ah yes, we were just stargazing and talking, but I suppose it's late," Mr. Johnson answered, readying himself to get up.

"We were just talking about the last time we attended a party like tonight," Mrs. Johnson interjected. "It was our son's wedding, and we all realized too late that we hadn't hired a clean-up crew. So, there we were, in our fancy outfits cleaning the reception hall." Mrs. Johnson laughed at the memory.

Diana giggled.

"Poor Claire, our daughter-in-law, got a wedding night she won't forget, in the worst way," Mr. Johnson added, chuckling.

Mrs. Johnson snorted with laughter at her husband's comment.

"Ah, but even though it's hilarious, we're really not so bad. We paid for them to go on a three-week honeymoon in the Seychelles to make up for it," Mrs. Johnson justified.

"Oh yes, that cost a pretty penny," Mr. Johnson recalled as his face regained a more serious expression. "It's a beautiful cluster of islands, just off the African coast. And it's warm all year round because it's an equatorial region," he added.

"Have you ever been there, Diana?" Mrs. Johnson asked.

Diana smiled and shook her head. "No, I haven't traveled much," the old detective admitted. "My career was the focal point of my life, and while I'm grateful to have seen most of this country, I haven't been elsewhere."

Mr. Johnson smiled kindly. "Ah, but there are plenty of stunning sites right here in the USA."

"Oh yes," Mrs. Johnson added. "A couple of years back, we took a month-long road trip. We explored many fascinating locations."

Diana enjoyed their conversation. They seemed sincere. The topics varied from special memories and occasions to more general elements.

The couple spoke about their three children, who all lived abroad now. They told her about their travels and interesting things that occurred in their lives.

After a while, the conversation faded into a comfortable silence, and the three sat gazing at the stars on a cloudless night.

"It's been a good life, hasn't it, Grace?" Mr. Johnson whispered lovingly, breaking the silence.

Mrs. Johnson nodded. "Oh yes, it has. Plenty of ups and downs, no doubt, but it's been an incredible journey. I wouldn't want to have shared it with anyone else."

A single tear formed in Mr. Johnson's eye.

"Diana, thank you. Thank you for an absolutely amazing night," Mrs. Johnson said sincerely as she placed her hand on Diana's.

The retired detective turned to face her and smiled. "You are most welcome, Mrs. Johnson. I'm honored to have been a part of such a special and exciting moment in your lives."

"I guess we all best get to bed then," Mr. Johnson finally said, getting up from his chair. "That is enough mushy talk for one night," he added with a soft chuckle.

Diana and Mrs. Johnson giggled.

"Oh yes, it will be another 40 years before I get another sentimental sentence out of him," Mrs. Johnson teased.

Mr. Johnson sighed. "I save it for the moments that matter." Then, he winked. The three went inside.

Diana made sure to close and lock all the doors. She finally made her way up the stairs and to her room. She felt good after the chat. It was a heartwarming conversation.

She decided that the Johnsons couldn't be to blame for the strange events. She even felt guilty for suspecting the elderly couple.

The retired detective took a warm shower and got into a comfortable pair of gray sweatpants and a t-shirt.

Suddenly, she remembered that someone had been in her room the previous night. As a precaution, she locked her door.

What bothered her the most was that whoever the intruder was, they didn't cause Sparky or Rover any alarm. That means it has to be someone they know.

Rover was asleep on her bed, so she snuggled up next to him and closed her eyes. She was exhausted, but she couldn't fall asleep.

She couldn't help but wonder about everything.

All these occurrences happened after my last batch of guests arrived. These people have no connection to each other, so it can't be a group effort. It has to be one of them. Elliot admitted that he's scouting the competition, but he wasn't the one causing the prints.

Mr. and Mrs. Johnson are in town to reminisce about the past and enjoy their 40th anniversary in the town where they met. They seem too sincere to be the culprits.

Amy has been outspoken and helpful from the first day here. She's an open book and keen to get to the bottom of the mystery too. I don't think it could be her.

Bobby's been working here since I opened the B&B. I trust him. It can't be him. Can it?

Diana's mind worked overtime. Everyone was a potential suspect, but almost everyone seemed like they couldn't be to blame either.

The retired detective tried to put all the pieces of the puzzle together. Her thoughts blurred, and she started dozing off. Then, with a gasp, she bolted upright.

"Mr. Franklin!" she uttered to herself. *It made sense. He was reclusive, only spoke about what was necessary, and nobody knows why he is in town. He also didn't seem too shaken when the footprints appeared.*

If it was Mr. Franklin, why had he left her the clue about the attic? Why sneak into her room and take the necklace? And how would he know about a secret passage when she didn't even know about it?

Diana decided that she'd have a friendly chat with him at breakfast. Perhaps she could pick up a few clues.

Soon her mind settled, and sleep engulfed her. She slept peacefully throughout the night.

The morning seemed to come too quickly. Diana turned off her alarm and excitedly checked her phone. Miriam would be arriving later that day. She texted her friend.

Diana: Good morning, Miriam. Safe travels. I can't wait to see you.

Then, she hopped out of bed and picked an outfit for the day. She decided on a pink and black summer dress that sat above her ankles.

Then she combed her hair and placed it in a bun at the crown of her head. She got ready for the day to the sweet sounds of birds tweeting outside her window.

Then she tidied up her room and made her way downstairs.

It was still early, but Diana decided to get breakfast ready. She flipped through the pages of her recipe book. She wanted to make something different.

"Hmmm, Belgian waffles," she thought aloud.

After a few minutes, she made up her mind and scuffled around the kitchen, getting all the ingredients. She was running short on a couple of items after the previous night's feast.

She placed two pans on her four-plate stove. She cracked several eggs in one and placed breakfast sausages in the other.

Then she prepared a batch of her famous cheesy hash browns. They were a bit unconventional, but her guests always complimented her on the flavor.

While the fried goods were sizzling on the stove, she whipped up a rich batter for chocolate Belgian waffles. The plan was to top them with rich homemade vanilla ice cream and juicy berries.

She glanced at her pantry. She felt as if she needed to add something else.

Then she smiled. "Of course!" she announced. "Fresh fruit platters."

The retired detective cut up a variety of fruits, expertly placing them in an attractive display. The arrangement consisted of blueberries, raspberries, chunks of pineapple, thinly sliced apples, and bananas. She made three platters and took them to the dining area.

"Good morning Bobby," she greeted him as he opened the door.

"Hi, Miss D," he responded.

"I'm surprised you're in so early. Last night was quite a late one."

Bobby replied, "I value this job. It's bad enough I missed a day this week."

Diana smiled. "Help yourself to a Belgian waffle and a cup of coffee in the kitchen. It's the first time I tried that recipe, and it seems like I've made far too many."

Bobby went to the kitchen, and Diana set the plates and cutlery on each of the tables. Mr. Franklin was the first to come downstairs.

Diana took a deep breath. She knew she had to be tactful. He was still her guest, after all.

"Good morning Mr. Franklin," she greeted him cheerfully.

"Hello, Diana," he responded with a smile. "Have you got another scrumptious feast lined up for us?"

The retired detective smiled politely, "I believe so. I hope you like Belgian waffles."

"Oh, that does sound good, but I'll admit I wanted something savory to start off with."

"Then you won't be disappointed," Diana remarked.

Just then, Bobby emerged from the kitchen. He was carrying trays of food to the buffet table.

"Will you be checking out after breakfast?" she asked as she filled his mug with coffee.

"Oh my. I've forgotten to request another extension," he gasped, and his eyes widened.

"What do you mean?" Diana asked.

"Well, my business in town is not quite complete," he said with a grave tone. "I wanted to stay an extra night if that's possible."

The retired detective's stomach churned. She felt uneasy but retained her calm demeanor.

"Sure, I can accommodate that," she responded cheerfully. "I didn't know you had a business here."

She played it cool, hoping he would give her some indication of why he was in town.

"No. I don't have business here. I just have business to do. Private matters and such," he answered coldly.

Diana nodded.

Elliot made his way down the stairs and greeted everyone.

"Diana, can I please have some coffee?" he requested.

"Of course, Elliot," she replied warmly and moved toward his table.

Something about Mr. Franklin didn't sit right with her.

Chapter 9

"Diana, what have you got planned for lunch?" Amy questioned while scarfing down the last of her Belgian waffle.

"Well," the B&B owner hesitated. "I'm not quite sure yet. I hope that you're not still hungry?" She teased.

"No, I was just thinking that we might have a relaxing barbeque," Amy suggested.

"That would be fun," Mr. Johnson piped in. "I haven't been to a barbeque in a good long while."

"I agree," Mrs. Johnson added.

Diana let out a nervous laugh. "A barbeque?"

"I'd enjoy that. Having our meal outdoors last night was refreshing. I'd like to do it again before we leave," Mr. Franklin added.

Diana shook her head and smiled. "Well, it's not a conventional B&B lunch. What are your thoughts, Elliot?"

"Oh, well, I won't be here for lunch," he answered awkwardly.

The room fell silent as everyone pondered his statement.

"I'm meeting a realtor," he added as he pursed his lips.

Diana knew what this meant. Elliot deemed the town a suitable fit for a holiday resort.

Not wanting to add discomfort, she nodded.

"I guess majority rules then. A barbeque it is!" Diana announced.

Her guests cheered.

After breakfast, Diana went upstairs and tried to contact Miriam.

Diana: Hi Miriam, I hope you're alright. I've tried calling you a couple of times. Pop me a text when you stop for gas or something. We're having a barbeque for lunch. See you soon.

Diana plugged her cell phone into its charger and wondered about the secret passage. She knew most of her guests would be out until lunchtime. But she wasn't sure where Bobby would be. She didn't want him to find the hidden door.

She took out the necklace key and considered inspecting the passage again. She walked toward the painting, but before she could remove it, she heard footsteps.

"Miss D, I have to pop out for a bit if that's okay? I need to get a couple of items for the barbeque," Bobby said.

"No problem Bobby. I might pop out for a bit myself in a little while. If you're back, and the front door is locked, know that I'll be back by 11:30."

Bobby nodded and hurried back down the stairs. Diana waited for a few minutes and then locked the door from the inside. She didn't want to risk anyone finding out about the passage until she knew more herself.

Carefully, she placed the shovel in the indentation, and the secret door in the wall opened like before. This time, Diana had a flashlight. She removed the lantern from the hook so that the passageway would close behind her.

Diana shone the flashlight on the staircase. She knew that she had about two hours to explore and wanted to soak up every detail so she could piece together the puzzle of this mystery.

She examined the staircase. It was expertly crafted. Diana felt that it was an architectural marvel.

The craftsman had used sturdy stone for the steps and wrought iron for the balustrades and banisters, and handrails. It was broad enough to allow one person to move comfortably.

When Diana reached the bottom of the spiral, she shone her flashlight toward it. There was a solid stone wall behind the stairs.

She followed the path ahead that led to the hidden room. It was dusty, but the place had clearly received plenty of foot traffic. Diana listened for any movement or voices, but it was quiet.

Finally, she reached the hidden room. She was sure that the sofa was part of the set her grandmother used to own.

Perhaps it was stolen.

She ran her fingers over the dust-covered shelf and recognized some of the books. Many of them were her grandmother's favorites. Others were cowboy-themed novels.

There were colorful cushions scattered on the floor and a few stuffed animals. They looked like the kind you could win at a carnival.

None of it made sense to Diana. She sat on the sofa and tried to figure out what she was missing. As she sat down, she felt something cold against her back.

She jumped up and shone her flashlight at the spot where she sat.

"A key?" she whispered.

The base of it was poking out from behind the backrest. She slowly pulled it out and inspected it.

It was a large, heavy old fashioned relic made of solid brass. The shaft was elongated. Diana caressed it and assessed how the jagged teeth of the biting were uniquely shaped. The whole key had indentations and imperfections.

It piqued the retired detective's curiosity.

"What do you open?" she questioned as she looked at it curiously.

Examining the room once more, Diana came to the conclusion that whatever the key opened wasn't in this room.

She returned to the secret passage. She considered going back to the B&B but decided to venture further into the darkness.

What other secrets lay within these walls?

Diana pondered the mystery as she walked.

The path narrowed, but she could still follow it comfortably. It felt like twenty minutes had passed when she caught a glimmer of light in the distance.

She was heading toward it when she noticed another door in the wall. It held a large candle.

Diana inhaled. *Perhaps this is where Old Smithy hid his treasure.*

She tried the handle. It was locked.

"That's what this is for!" she whispered to herself as she pushed the key in.

It turned.

"Bingo," she said excitedly.

She opened the door, and heaps of gray dirt instantly fell out. Diana coughed profusely and moved out of the way.

Once the dirt settled, she looked inside. There was nothing but massive gray rocks and rubble that blocked her view.

"They must have closed this for a reason," she said aloud. Then, the retired detective forced the old door shut, locked it, and continued toward the light.

When she saw she was only a few feet away from the light, she recognized her surroundings. She was in the old mine.

It was one of the passages Old Smithy had declared unsafe. By now, Diana was out of breath.

The retired detective took a few minutes to catch her breath, then made her way back to Bakers Inn. She enjoyed her little walk but still had no answers.

Perhaps it was Elliot that opened the passageway. We did find him in the mine by himself that day.

Diana's thoughts kept running through her mind. She had hundreds of suspicions but no concrete evidence.

"Come on now, girl, you're grasping at straws," she scolded herself as she put the lantern back on the hook on the wall. The secret door slid open as she anticipated, and she stepped back into the lobby.

Then she straightened the painting and saw that her fingers left black marks on the frame.

"I have to clean that off. Right after I clean myself up," she mumbled, noticing that she and her summer dress were covered in dust.

She checked the time. "11 o'clock. That gives me enough time to shower and do meal preparations for the barbeque."

Diana showered and washed her hair. She opted for light blue jeans and a white satin shirt. It was a hot day, so she left her hair to air dry. Soft curls formed and framed her face beautifully.

The retired detective first cleaned the dusty prints from the frame of the painting before rushing downstairs to unlock the front door. Then, she headed to the kitchen.

She rummaged through her cupboards, looking for the barbeque utensils.

Suddenly, She felt Peaches rubbing against her ankles, and she reached down to pet her soft fur.

"Hi, darling," Diana smiled. "I must look a bit silly, bustling about like this, I know." She giggled.

After finding everything she needed, Diana marinated the chicken and prepared a variety of salads.

Diana cut up different kinds of vegetables and placed them on skewers for grilling.

"Hey, Miss D, I think I've managed to get everything we need," Bobby announced with his hands full of shopping bags.

Diana laughed. "You startled me, Bobby. I got so busy; I didn't even hear you come in."

"Do you want me to start setting up outside?" he responded.

Diana nodded. "Yes, please use the same tables and chairs we used last night."

The B&B owner knew exactly what she wanted to prepare for dessert. It was tradition. Whenever her parents had a barbeque, she knew that she could look forward to a mouth-watering apple pie and some brownies for dessert.

She started with the applesauce when her phone started buzzing. She reached into her pocket. It was a text from Miriam.

Miriam: Hi Diana, sorry for only responding now. Some places had patchy reception. I should be there by 2:30 pm, so I might miss lunch. Save me something yummy, will you? Can't wait to see you!

Diana was happy her friend would be there soon.

She finished with her preparations, set a timer, and popped the pie into the oven.

"Miss D, I think everything is set up. Can I help with anything here?" Bobby questioned, sticking his head through the door.

"Yes, please. The meat is all ready for you to grill, and you can take a large jar of lemonade to each table." she replied.

Should I take the sodas out, too?" he asked.

"Well, let's wait a bit and leave them in the fridge to keep cold."

Soon enough, everyone except Amy was gathered in the back garden while Bobby grilled hotdogs and burgers.

Everyone was cheerful and talking about the previous night.

Diana was nervously waiting for Amy and Old Smithy's grandson to arrive. She desperately wanted to get to the bottom of everything and hoped that their meeting would yield some answers.

Most of the guests were enjoying their meal when Amy and Steven finally got there. They walked up to Diana.

Steven wasn't what she had imagined him to be. He appeared to be in his late 50s, a handsome, rugged man with green eyes and slicked black silver hair. He wore a crisp white shirt, blue jeans, and brown leather boots.

"Diana, this is Steven, Old Smithy's eldest grandson," Amy introduced them.

"Pleased to meet you," the B&B owner responded.

"I heard that you're quite curious about my grandfather's legend."

Diana felt uncomfortable. "Well, I'd like to learn more about him." She replied.

Steven smiled kindly. "Most of the rumors aren't true, of course. But I was promised a meal in exchange for the information I'm about to divulge," he teased.

"Oh yes, definitely," Diana answered, feeling more comfortable. "Have a seat, and Bobby will bring over some burgers and hotdogs from the grill."

"Please join us," Steven requested. "I do my best talking with my mouth full." He jested.

Diana giggled. "Of course. Be sure to try the potato salad. I've been told it's a hit."

The trio sat at the table closest to the pool, and Amy and Diana looked at Steven in anticipation.

Their guest took a big bite of his burger and finally spoke.

"His name was Olden Smith. That's why the legend is about Old Smithy. It's not because he was old," he said.

Diana and Amy exchanged glances.

"See, that's one rumor put to rest," he laughed. "In all seriousness, my grandfather was an old-fashioned, hard-working, kind man. He became a widow at a young age and channeled his grief into his work."

Diana listened attentively.

"He believed that if you work real hard, eventually, any emotional hurt leaves. He was generous and loving and tried to give his children the best that he could." Steven smiled as he reminisced.

"Do you remember him?" Amy asked.

"I have faint memories. I was 5 when he passed away. He spent most of his life in that mine, and he died there too. It was a terrible accident.

Most folks think he haunts the place or that they never retrieved his body. But we did, and we had a private funeral and everything," he explained.

"Wow. So, where did the rumors come from?" Amy questioned.

Steven shrugged. "It's a small town, people gossip. He liked to keep things private, and we respected that. There was nothing greedy or crazy about him. Working just helped him keep his mind off his grief. Until he finally stopped grieving."

"When was that?" Amy asked.

Steven indeed deeply. "Many, many years later. By that time, working hard had become habitual for him, but I'm glad to know that when he did pass away, he was happy." He finished.

"Thank you for sharing that with us," Diana replied.

"And thank you for lunch. I must be on my way now," he announced as he got up from his chair and left.

Diana felt more puzzled than ever. She started cleaning up the tables and taking dishes to the kitchen when she heard an all too familiar voice.

"Diana, I'm here," Miriam announced as she entered the front door.

She didn't have much luggage, just a simple overnight bag, and her purse.

The retired detective set down the plates and rushed to embrace her dear old friend.

"Miriam, I am so glad that you're here!" she exclaimed. "It's been the craziest week. I'll take you up to your room, and after that, there's something I must show you."

Chapter 10

Diana had just finished putting a large casserole into the oven for dinner.

"Bobby, keep an eye on this, would you?"

Her assistant nodded with a smile.

"Would you mind serving dinner tonight? Aside from the casserole, there are sauteed mushrooms, roasted potatoes, steamed corn, and salad. Dessert is Miriam's favorite—sweet potato pie. Everything is already prepared. All you have to do is take the casserole out in 10 minutes."

"No problem Miss D. I'll handle everything. Your friend has come a long way to see you," Bobby answered kindly.

"Thank you, Bobby," she replied before making her way upstairs.

KNOCK! KNOCK! KNOCK!

"Come in," Miriam called.

Diana entered the room and sat on the bed next to her friend.

"You must be quite tired after such a long trip. I saved you some apple pie, and there are a couple of burgers too."

Miriam smiled. "I've missed you. I'll definitely enjoy those treats a bit later. Right now, I'm curious to know what you want to show me."

The B&B owner reached into her jeans pocket and removed the necklace.

"I found this necklace in the attic," she whispered.

"It's a pretty unique piece of jewelry, Di," Miriam commented.

Diana smirked. "It opens a secret passage," she added, knowing it would get her friend curious.

"You're joking," Miriam replied.

The retired detective shook her head. Her eyes were wide with excitement. She was so glad to have someone to share this information with. Perhaps Miriam would help her solve it; they made a pretty good detective team for many years.

"Let me see it," Miriam requested.

Diana nodded, and the pair made their way to the lobby. She lifted the painting, inserted the pendant, and the secret door in the wall opened.

"What???" Miriam exclaimed in disbelief.

"You'll need this. It gets pretty dark in there," Diana explained, passing an extra flashlight to her friend.

As they entered, Diana removed the lantern from the hook, and the secret door in the wall closed behind them.

"Oh, my word," Miriam gasped. "Wait, are those stairs?" she inquired, shining her flashlight ahead.

"Yes, it goes down pretty far," Diana warned.

"What's that sound?" Miriam asked.

There was a soft shuffling sound, and just then, Diana felt something run over her foot.

"AAAH!" screamed the B&B owner dropping the lantern.

"It's a rat," Miriam commented as she shone the flashlight at the scampering rodent.

The pair burst out laughing, and Diana bent down to pick up the lantern. It wasn't too badly damaged, although it was dented on one side.

"I'm all for exploring, but let me change into a pair of closed shoes before we venture down there," said Miriam.

"I agree," Diana chuckled.

They turned back, and she hung the lantern on the hook. Surprisingly, the secret door in the wall didn't open. Perhaps it was because the lantern was damaged.

She removed it and tried again. Still, the wall remained in place.

"What's going on, Diana?" Miriam asked.

"We're stuck."

"What do you mean we're stuck?" Miriam questioned with concern.

"I usually just hang the lantern on the hook, and the secret door opens," Diana explained.

The retired detective then tried pulling on the hook with her fingers but had no luck opening the door.

"Diana, we can't spend the night here," Miriam uttered.

The B&B owner thought for a moment and then said, "There's another way out through the old, abandoned mine."

"Fantastic. How far is it?" Miriam asked.

Diana sighed. "It's about a 20-minute walk."

"Let's hurry then."

The two friends cautiously climbed down the stairs and then walked briskly down the path.

"See, here's the hidden room where I found Mittens," said Diana, shining the flashlight into the arched door.

"How odd to have a secret room in the middle of nowhere," Miriam replied.

The duo continued walking right up to where the path got narrow.

"It will be a tight squeeze, but the mine exit is only a few feet away," Diana explained.

Miriam nodded.

They finally reached the place where the mine tours started, but the gates were shut. There was no way out.

"Maybe if we yell?" Miriam suggested.

Diana wasn't so sure.

"Help! Anyone? Help! We're in here! We're in the mine!" Miriam called out.

There was no response.

"Oh, Miriam, I'm so sorry," Diana apologized. "I was so excited to show you what I'd discovered; I didn't for a minute think we'd be trapped."

Both friends felt panicked, but as seasoned detectives that had seen their share of danger, they maintained calm dispositions.

"It's okay, Diana. Let's head back to that hidden room before our flashlights go out," Miriam replied nervously.

The friends dusted out the cushions of the sofa and tried to get comfortable for the night.

"This was not how I imagined my first night at your B&B," Miriam joked.

Diana laughed. "What do you mean? This is five-star accommodation."

The pair turned their flashlights off to save the batteries. Then they talked and laughed as if they weren't trapped in an underground hidden room.

After a while, they heard a noise. It sounded like footsteps coming toward them. They also saw a light in the distance that seemed to be getting closer.

Unsure of whether the person approaching was friend or foe, they decided to remain quiet.

"Diana? Are you here?" the unknown person called. It was a powerful masculine voice.

Not knowing what to make of the situation, the friends remained silent.

"Diana, it's Steven. Are you in here?" he called out again.

The retired detective took a deep breath. "Yes, Steven, we're in here," she responded.

"Do you know this person?" Miriam whispered, concerned that she'd just given up their whereabouts.

"Kind of. We met yesterday," Diana answered.

Steven's light got brighter as he entered the room. He smiled. "I'm so glad you're both okay," he panted, clearly out of breath from searching.

"What are you doing here, Steven?" Diana questioned. She was both afraid and relieved.

"I saw the lamp was broken, so I figured you must be stuck down here," he answered matter of factly. "The hooks are weight sensitive. I'll measure it out and have it fixed for you."

The B&B owner's eyes grew wide.

"Before you panic, let me explain," Steven began. He grabbed a large blue cushion and sat on the floor in front of them.

"This is Old Smithy's treasure. This room, the secret passage, and your B&B," he announced. "My grandfather built all of this so he could keep his companionship with your grandmother, Hannah, discreet."

"What?" Diana asked in shock.

"Your grandmother was widowed early, just like my grandfather. They met a few times and eventually formed a friendship that blossomed into something more. But in a small town, people started gossiping. So, he built these pathways deep within the mine. Here they'd meet and talk and spend time without prying eyes."

"Wait... what do you mean the B&B is part of his treasure?" Diana marveled.

"When your father went to college, they had to take a second mortgage on the house. Years later, as an aging widow, she struggled to afford the payments. Your grandmother was left to pay the bills all by herself. My grandfather helped her settle it without anyone knowing. It was his gift to her."

"There's no way that's true," Diana gasped.

"Let me show you," Steven responded.

He carefully moved the bookshelf and revealed a hole in the wall with a small chest inside.

He pulled it out and opened it with a brass key similar to the one Diana found.

"Have a look. It's a bunch of photographs. There are also love letters, short notes, and all kinds of memorabilia," he commented.

Diana rummaged through the items and inspected some of the photographs. "So, it's true," she said in astonishment.

Miriam remained silent.

"He asked her to marry him, you know, and he engraved the words "Hannah Smith" on the key in hopes of her saying yes one day," Steven added.

"Did she?" Diana asked.

"Yes, but he died before they could announce it to anyone," Steven replied. "And that's all of it. That's the mystery of Old Smithy."

Diana was in disbelief.

"Why haven't I been told any of this?" she inquired.

"When Old Smithy died, rumors spread. Your grandmother knew the truth and didn't want her family to be dragged into unnecessary gossip. My father knew the truth and kept it private, but when I got older and asked him about the stories, he told me everything and showed me this place."

"This is a lot of information to take in at once," Diana stated.

"How will we get out of here?" Miriam finally asked.

Steven smiled. "Follow me."

The three followed the path but took a different turn than the mine exit. It felt as if they'd been walking for an hour when they finally reached the door.

Steven placed a small bucket of water on a hook, similar to the one that opened the secret door at the B&B. The weight caused a door to open into his garage.

"This is my home. It used to be my grandfather's," he explained. "I'll drive you back to the B&B."

"Thank you, Steven," Diana replied gratefully. She was still absorbing all the new information Steven divulged.

The drive back was mostly silent. Diana was surprised that the legend wasn't as dark as she'd expected.

When they pulled up in front of her home, Steven walked them to the front door. It was quiet inside.

Finally, Diana's curiosity got the best of her. "So, why now? Why did you choose to share all this with me? Why the footprints?"

Steven smiled. "Because you missed sleuthing."

Diana's eyes grew wide. The only person she'd told was Miriam.

She glanced at her friend, who tried hard to conceal a smirk.

"This was all you?" Diana asked.

"You said you missed it, so I sent Wayne and Ruby to scout things out. It turns out you had a massive mystery right under your nose. Ruby then contacted Steven to sprinkle some clues around the B&B," Miriam explained with a twinkle in her eye.

Steven opened the front door, and all Diana's guests stood in the hall clapping and cheering. They had bought a massive three-tiered cake, which said, "Congratulations Diana." Even Sparky, Rover, Peaches, and Mittens were present for the festivities.

"We wanted to help you feel like yourself again," chimed Amy as she took off her wig and prosthetic nose.

"Agatha? From the main office?" Diana questioned.

"At your service," she replied happily.

One by one, each of her guests removed their disguises. They were all previous co-workers.

Diana chuckled. "Oh, you guys! This was such an amazing gesture."

"There is no big holiday resort," Elliot, who was actually Michael, announced. "I was working on creating a website for this place. That anniversary party you threw for Ruby and Wayne was ideal for the section of the site that says you host events."

Diana had a massive smile on her face. She couldn't believe all the trouble everyone had gone through to make her feel the joy of sleuthing.

"We'll all return home in the morning," Mr. Johnson, who was actually Wayne, commented.

"But the secret passage will still be there, and I'm happy to add some new footprints if you're longing for another mystery," Steven joked.

"Now let's cut this amazing cake and celebrate a decades-long mystery being solved," Miriam said happily.

Everyone laughed and cheered as they enjoyed their final feast together.

www.ingramcontent.com/pod-product-compliance
Lightning Source LLC
Chambersburg PA
CBHW031458130726
47989CB00003B/1447